GOODNIGHT STORIES
for the
Very Young

SELECTED BY SALLY GRINDLEY
• ILLUSTRATED BY CHRIS FISHER •

Kingfisher

For Gina S.G.
For Jannie C.F.

KINGFISHER
An imprint of Larousse plc
Elsley House, 24-30 Great Titchfield Street
London W1P 7AD

This edition published by Kingfisher 1995
2 4 6 8 10 9 7 5 3 1
This selection copyright © Sally Grindley 1994
Illustrations copyright © Chris Fisher 1991, 1994

The Way Out © Joyce Dunbar 1991
When Am I Going Home? © Sally Grindley 1991
Watch Out for Tusker © Sarah Hayes 1991
Norty Boy © Dick King-Smith 1991
Emily Hogg and Doctor Dog Go to the Ceiling © Sue Limb 1991
Baby Wizard © Chris Powling 1991

Material in this edition was previously published
by Kingfisher Books in hardback in 1991
in *Bedtime Stories for the Very Young*,
and in paperback in 1994 as *Goodnight
Stories for the Very Young*.

A CIP catalogue record for this book
is available from the British Library

ISBN 1 85697 340 9

Designed by Tony Potter
Printed in Hong Kong

Contents

EMILY HOGG AND DOCTOR DOG
GO TO THE CEILING   (*5 minutes*)
Sue Limb   4

NORTY BOY   (*5 minutes*)
Dick King-Smith   10

THE WAY OUT   (*4 minutes*)
Joyce Dunbar   17

BABY WIZARD   (*3 minutes*)
Chris Powling   21

WATCH OUT FOR TUSKER   (*4 minutes*)
Sarah Hayes   26

WHEN AM I GOING HOME?   (*5 minutes*)
Sally Grindley   32

EMILY HOGG AND DOCTOR DOG GO TO THE CEILING

Sue Limb

"Goodnight, my little egg," said Emily's Dad, and then he made a whistling sound: CHEWP CHEWP CHEWP TIRILEE.

"Goodnight, Big Bird," said Emily.

Emily was in a bird phase right now. Even her pyjama top had a pattern of yellow birds.

After her Dad had gone, Emily lay and looked at the ceiling. Up there above her head was a strange stain. Sometimes it looked like a lake, sometimes like an island. Sometimes it looked like a tree, and sometimes like an angry old man.

"What does that stain look like to you?" asked Emily. In bed with her was Doctor Dog – her cuddliest, oldest toy.

"Wow! It looks just like a bone!" he barked. "Let's go and see! Hold tight for take-off!"

There was a whirring sound, and Emily's bed rose up in the air as if it was a helicopter. Emily held on tight and watched her bedroom get smaller and further away, until the window was the size of a tiny fingernail.

"Ladies 'n' Gentlemen," announced Doctor Dog, flying the bedicopter very expertly into a wild blue wind, "you may unfasten your seatbelts."

Up ahead Emily saw a glittering lake getting bigger and bigger as they went towards it.

"Ah!" said Emily, "so it *is* a lake!"

In the middle of the lake was a tiny island.

"Oh no, it's an island after all!"

In the middle of the island was a tree.

"I see!" said Emily, "so it really is a *tree*! Can we land on that island, Doctor Dog?"

"Going in to land now," reported Doctor Dog. "Thirty . . . twenty . . . We have landed. A giant leap for dog kind." And he bounded out and frisked under the tree.

"Wow! What a great place! Throw me a stick, Emily!"

Emily wasn't so sure. There was something about the place that seemed sad. It was so silent and still. All the same, she reached up into the tree, broke off a little stick and threw it for Doctor Dog, way out into the lake. He plunged in after it. Everything seemed even quieter after he'd gone.

Emily looked into the tree, and saw some green apples hanging there. She picked up onc and sat down on a rock to eat it. But the first bite was so sour and awful, she threw it away into the lake. It made a sad PLOP sound which echoed into the stillness. Then suddenly a voice crackled out, sharp and deep.

"You steal my apples and then you throw them away! What sort of girl are you?"

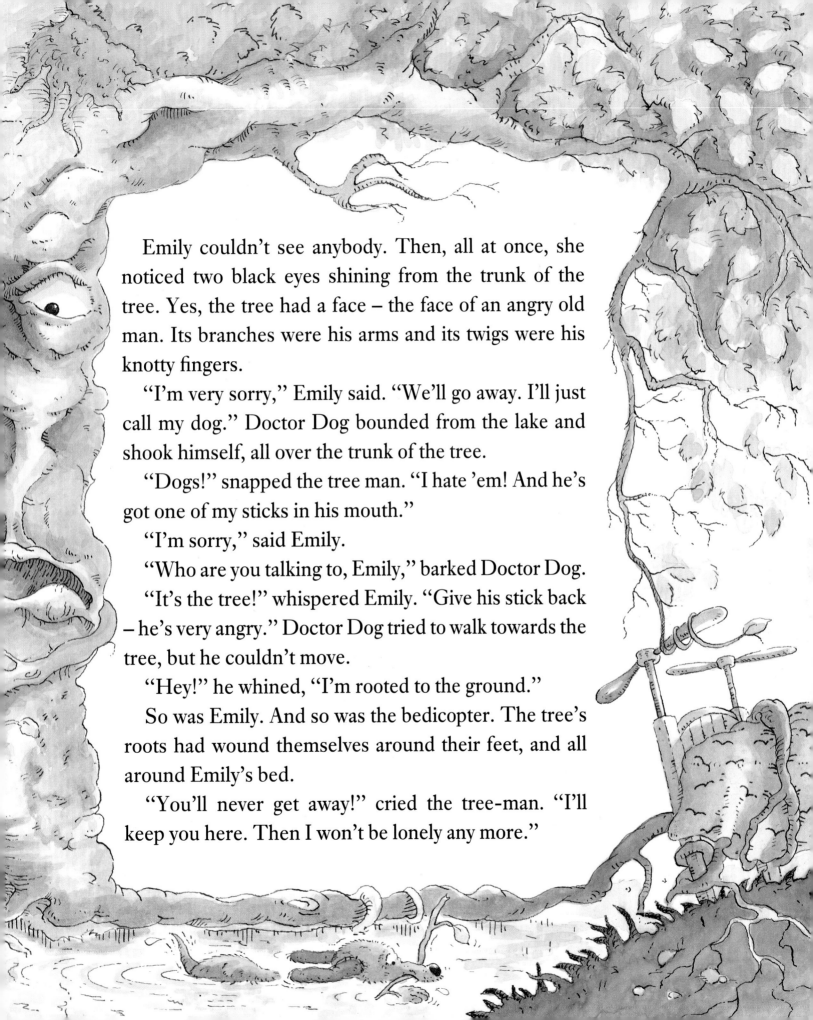

Emily couldn't see anybody. Then, all at once, she noticed two black eyes shining from the trunk of the tree. Yes, the tree had a face – the face of an angry old man. Its branches were his arms and its twigs were his knotty fingers.

"I'm very sorry," Emily said. "We'll go away. I'll just call my dog." Doctor Dog bounded from the lake and shook himself, all over the trunk of the tree.

"Dogs!" snapped the tree man. "I hate 'em! And he's got one of my sticks in his mouth."

"I'm sorry," said Emily.

"Who are you talking to, Emily," barked Doctor Dog.

"It's the tree!" whispered Emily. "Give his stick back – he's very angry." Doctor Dog tried to walk towards the tree, but he couldn't move.

"Hey!" he whined, "I'm rooted to the ground."

So was Emily. And so was the bedicopter. The tree's roots had wound themselves around their feet, and all around Emily's bed.

"You'll never get away!" cried the tree-man. "I'll keep you here. Then I won't be lonely any more."

Doctor Dog started to howl, and Emily was very near crying. Then she had an idea.

"I know why you're lonely!" she said. "Because you've got no birds! That's what a tree needs – birds!" And she pulled off her pyjama top. "Look!" she went on, "my pyjama top is covered with birds!" And she threw the pyjama top towards the tree.

As it flew, there was a sort of golden explosion and all the little yellow birds burst out of it in a brilliant cloud. They twittered and fluttered and perched on the branches of the tree.

"Cheep cheep cheep TIRILEE!"

Some began to build nests. Some sharpened their beaks on the branches. Suddenly the great green tree was full of music and life, and a slow grin spread across its gnarled old face. The roots uncoiled themselves from around Emily's ankles. She was free! And so were Doctor Dog and the bedicopter. Quickly waving

8

goodbye to the smiling tree, they took off and flew back home.

"Emily," said Emily's mother next day, "where's your pyjama top?"

"Oh," Emily began to explain, "you see the stain on the ceiling? Well, it's an old man, but he's a tree really, and he lives on an island, in the middle of a lake, and he needed the birds because he was so lonely, so I gave him my pyjama top."

"Well, that's a great story," said her mother, "but where's your pyjama top *really*?"

Emily sighed. There were some things grown-ups just didn't understand. Her mother went on looking for that pyjama top for a week and a day, even though Emily kept on telling her it was on the ceiling – and come to think of it, if you looked up at the stain, you could see the pyjama top clear as anything, along with the lake and the island and the old tree-man. And if the wind was in the right direction, you could even hear the birds sing.

NORTY BOY

Dick King-Smith

Hylda was an old-fashioned sort of animal. She did not hold with the free and easy ways of the modern hedgehog, and even preferred to call herself by the old name of 'hedgepig'. She planned to bring up her seven hedgepiglets very strictly.

'Children should be seen and not heard' was one of her favourite sayings, and 'Speak when you're spoken to' was another. She taught them to say 'Please' and 'Thank you', to eat nicely, to sniff quietly if their noses were running, and never to scratch in public, no matter how many fleas they had.

Six of them – three boys and three girls – grew up to be well-behaved, with beautiful manners, but the seventh was a great worry to Hylda and her husband Herbert. This seventh hedgepiglet was the despair of Hylda's life. He was not only seen but constantly heard, speaking whether he was spoken to or not, and he never said 'Please' or 'Thank you'. He gobbled his food in a revoltingly slobbery way, he sniffed very loudly indeed and he was forever scratching.

His real name was Norton, but he was more often known as Norty.

Now some mother animals can wallop their young ones if they do not do what they are told. A lioness can cuff her cub, a monkey can clip its child round the ear, or an elephant can give her baby a biff with her trunk. But it's not so easy for hedgehogs.

"Sometimes," said Hylda to Herbert. "I wish that hedgepigs didn't have prickles"

"Why is that, my dear?" said Herbert.

"Because then I could give our Norty a good hiding. He deserves it."

"Why is that, my dear?" said Herbert.

"Not only is he disobedient, he has taken to answering me back. Why can't he be good like the others? Never have I known such a hedgepiglet. I shall be glad when November comes."

"Why is that, my dear?" said Herbert.

"Because then it's time to hibernate, of course, and we can all have a good sleep. For five blissful months I shall not have to listen to that impudent, squeaky little voice arguing, complaining, refusing to do what I say and generally giving me cheek."

Hylda should have known it would not be that easy.

When November came, she said to her husband and the seven children, "Come along, all of you."

"Yes, Mummy," said the three good boys and the

three good girls, and "Why is that, my dear?" said Herbert, but Norty only said, "Shan't."

"Norty," said Hylda. "If you do not do what you are told, I shall get your father to give you a good hard smack."

Norty fluffed up his spines and sniggered.

"You'll be sorry if you do, Dad," he said.

"Where are we going, Mummy?" asked one of the hedgepiglets.

"We are going to find a nice deep bed of dry leaves, where we can hibernate."

"What does 'hibernate' mean, Mummy?" asked another.

"It means to go to sleep, all through the winter. When it's rainy and blowy and frosty and snowy outside, we shall all be fast asleep under the leaf pile, all cosy and warm. Won't that be lovely?"

"No," said Norty.

"Norton!" said his mother angrily. "Are you coming or are you not?"

"No," said Norty.

"Oh well, stay here then!" snapped Hylda. "And freeze to death!" and she trotted off with the rest.

In a far corner of the garden they found a nice deep bed of dry leaves, and Hylda and Herbert and the six good hedgepiglets burrowed their way into it, and curled up tight, and shut their eyes, and went to sleep.

The following April they woke up, and opened their eyes, and uncurled, and burrowed out into the Spring sunshine.

"Goodbye Mummy! Goodbye Daddy!" chorused the six good hedgepiglets, and off they trotted to seek their fortunes.

"Oh Herbert!" said Hylda. "I feel so sad."

"Why is that, my dear?" said Herbert.

"I should never have left our Norty out in the cold last November. He will have frozen to death, poor little fellow. What does it matter that he was rude and disobedient and cheeky? Oh, if only I could hear his squeaky voice again, I'd be the happiest hedgepig ever!"

At that moment there was a rustling from the other side of the bed of leaves, and out came Norty.

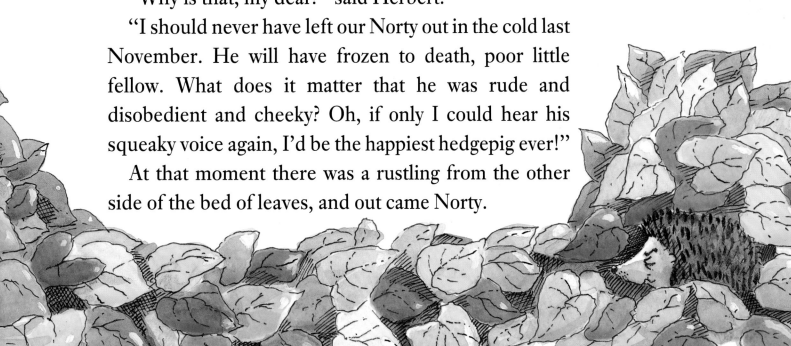

"Can't you keep your voices down?" he said, yawning. "A fellow can't get a wink of sleep."

"Oh Norty!" cried Hylda. "Come and give Mummy a kiss!"

"Shan't," said Norty.

"Aren't you pleased to see us?"

"No," said Norty.

At this Hylda completely lost her temper.

"Well, push off then!" she shouted. "Your brothers and sisters have all gone, so get lost!"

"Shan't," said Norty. "I'm going to stay with you, so there!"

"Oh no, you're not!" screamed Hylda. "You're the rudest hedgepig in the world and your father's the most boring, and I've had enough of both of you!" and she ran away as fast as she could go.

Herbert and Norty stared after her. Norty scratched his fleas and sniffed very noisily.

"Looks like she's done a bunk, Dad," he said.

"Yes," said Herbert. "Why is that, my dear?"

"Can't think," said Norty. "But then she always was prickly."

THE WAY OUT

Joyce Dunbar

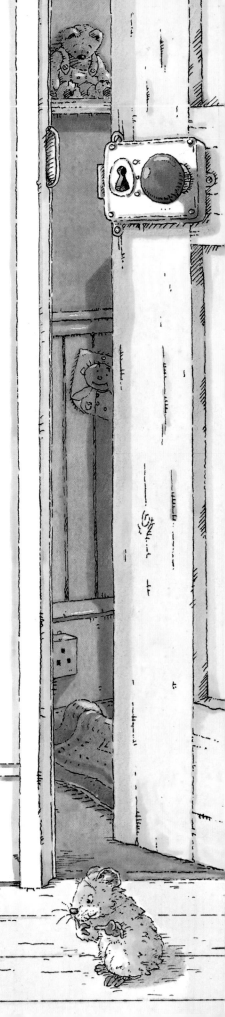

Thompson was a long-haired hamster. He was very clean and very curious. He belonged to a boy called Luke.

Thompson's cage was in Luke's bedroom. It was a good-sized cage, with an upstairs and a downstairs. It had a newspaper nest inside a sleeping compartment, drinking water in a bottle on the side, a wheel and two ladders.

Thompson slept all day, but when night time came he was up and about. He ran around his cage, up and down his ladders, round and round in his wheel. But that wasn't enough.

Thompson wanted to find the way out.

One night, after Luke had gone to bed, Thompson saw that his cage door was open! Thompson stayed still for a minute, sat on his hind legs, smartened up his whiskers and listened. He could feel the big room all around him!

He scrambled through the open door and toppled onto the bedroom floor. Across the carpet he scuttled, under the bed, into the cupboard, along the shelves, in and out of shoes, in between Luke's toys. But that still wasn't enough.

Thompson wanted to find the way out.

So he gnawed at the skirting board and scraped at the floorboards. He sniffed at the gap by the door then managed to squeeze his way through. Thompson stayed still for a moment, pricked up his ears and listened. He could feel the big house all around him!

Through the bedrooms he ran, in and out of the bathroom, before scrambling all the way downstairs. He went into the living room, behind the sofa, in and out of drawers, under the door into the kitchen. Even so, that wasn't enough.

Thompson wanted to find the way out.

Then he smelt something through the cat-flap in the door. Fresh air! He flipped through onto the path outside. There he stayed still for a moment, took a deep breath and listened. He could feel the big town all around him!

Across the garden he ran, through the gate, all along the street, past the shops and schools, until he reached the middle of the town. Even so, that wasn't enough.

Thompson wanted to find the way out.

Then he saw a bus waiting at the bus-stop.

Thompson stayed still for a moment, cocked his head on one side and listened. He could sense the big country all around him!

So he stowed away on the bus and went through villages, towns and cities. He hopped on and off trains which took him up and down dale. He ran through forests and over fields until he came to the edge of the land. Yet still that wasn't enough.

Thompson wanted to find the way out.

Then he saw the wide open sea. Thompson sat still for a moment, polished his nose with his paws and listened. He could feel the great world all around him!

So he stowed away on a ship, to the North Pole and the South Pole. And he stowed away on aeroplanes to the East and to the West. Soon he had been right around the world! But it just wasn't enough.

Thompson wanted to find the way out.

He looked up at the great empty sky. Thompson sat still for a moment, heaved a big sigh and listened. He could feel outer space all above him!

So he stowed away on a rocket to the moon. He ran all around the moon, in and out of craters. Then he jumped onto a shooting star which took him to the edge of the universe.

He peeped over the edge of the universe. He saw an endless big black hole!

E-E-E-K!

Thompson had had quite enough. He wanted to find the way home.

Thompson sat still for a moment, stood on his hind legs and suddenly felt very dizzy. He covered his eyes with his paws and fell into the big black hole.

Down and down he went, very fast and far, until he landed with a very soft bump.

Thompson uncovered his eyes. He was back inside Luke's room.

"Where have you been?" cried Luke. "I've been looking everywhere for you!" Luke picked him up and stroked him and put him back inside his cage, with an upstairs and a downstairs and a wheel and two ladders.

Thompson sat still for a moment, then he had some biscuit for breakfast and a drink from his bottle. He smoothed down his fur and curled up in his newspaper nest.

How cosy and sleepy he felt! How very safe and sound!

BABY WIZARD

Chris Powling

Once there was a Baby Wizard.

Her Dad was a wizard, her Mum was a wizard and so was her big brother, aged five, who'd just started Wizard School. They lived in a spiky-towered castle with a deep, dark forest all round it – which is just where you'd expect a wizard family to live.

One thing you wouldn't expect, though. *This* Baby Wizard was special. She couldn't walk yet. She couldn't talk yet. She couldn't feed herself yet – and she certainly couldn't use her potty.

BUT SHE COULD MAKE MAGIC!

At first, of course, the family didn't believe it.

"Impossible," said her Dad. "Wizards must learn how to make magic – no one can be magical while they're still wearing a nappy!"

Baby Wizard could.

"Goo-goo-goo," she said. And instantly she turned

her pram into a racing car that roared straight down the motorway as far as the big city. Her Mum and Dad were furious when they had to collect her from the police station.

Mealtimes were even worse. Sometimes Baby Wizard turned her food into rubber so it bounced all over the castle kitchen. Sometimes she made it so heavy it fell to the floor with a CRASH that shook the whole forest. Sometimes she floated it out of the window, so it hung high over the castle like a tiny, food-coloured cloud.

At bathtimes she was even naughtier – filling the bath with crocodiles, for instance.

"Crocodiles?" shrieked Mum, snatching Baby Wizard from the water. "She's too little even to have heard of crocodiles!"

"Goo-goo-goo," said Baby Wizard. And the crocodiles changed into dragons so fiery they nearly

burnt the bathroom to bits with their breath.

Naturally, all this was a great nuisance – but nothing more than a nuisance. Remember, every member of her family was a wizard. They could always put things right with plenty of magic of their own.

The real problem came at bedtime.

Bedtime, yes.

Her Mum and Dad and her big brother, aged five, were too terrified now to go to sleep. Night after night they lay awake wondering what Baby Wizard would get up to after dark.

"Suppose it's a magic sneeze!" exclaimed her Dad. "She might blow away the whole forest!"

"Suppose it's a magic burp!" cried Mum. "She might split the castle in two like an earthquake!"

"Suppose it's a magic nightmare!" yelled her big brother, aged five. "She might fill every corner of the forest with gho-gho-gho-ghosts!"

Even when they took turns to watch over Baby Wizard's cot it didn't help. They were still so scared of what might happen none of them shut their eyes for a moment.

"This is terrible," yawned Baby Wizard's Mum. "I can't remember when we last had a good night's sleep."

"We're falling to bits from tiredness," Dad groaned. "Isn't there anything we can do?"

Baby Wizard's big brother, aged five, looked down at his little sister in her cot and scratched his head thoughtfully.

"Dad," he said. "Can a kitten do magic?"

"A kitten?"

"Or a puppy?"

"A puppy?"

"Or a chick? Or a calf? Or a piglet?"

"Of course not," Dad Wizard said. "Only a wizard can do magic – you learn how at Wizard School. Or so I thought till your sister came along."

"That's what I thought," said Baby Wizard's big brother, aged five. "So now I've got the answer to our problem!"

Quickly he waggled his fingers and muttered a magic word.

"Miaow-miaow-miaow," went Baby Wizard in her sleep. Then "purr-purr-purr".

Baby Wizard's big brother, aged five, had turned her into a kitten!

Every bedtime after that, Baby Wizard licked her whiskers, curled her tail and purred herself to sleep till morning . . . except, of course, when she'd been turned into a puppy or a chick or a calf or a piglet.

And her family slept happily ever after.

Especially her big brother, aged five, who'd just started Wizard School. Some people say that by the time he's grown up he'll be the best wizard ever . . . unless, of course, his sister is just as good.

WATCH OUT FOR TUSKER

Sarah Hayes

Tess stared crossly at the raindrops making rivers on her window pane. She didn't want to play inside. Her room was a mess. Tess kicked a brick under the bed. Clonk! The brick hit something that wasn't the wall. Tess knelt down to have a look, and then she remembered the toy-box Dad had fetched from the loft. His old cars were in there, all scratched and battered. Tess had pushed the box under her bed and forgotten about it. Now she pulled it out.

The box was heavy. She took off the lid and looked inside. The cars weren't very interesting, but there were other things underneath, done up in tissue paper. Tess unwrapped one of the packages: it was a painted metal horse with big feet. It wasn't scratched or battered like the cars. Tess weighed the horse in her hand. It was heavier than the animals you get nowadays. She unwrapped another package. Five ducklings fell on to the carpet. Tess had found Dad's old farm.

There were horses and cows and sheep and lambs and dogs and cats and ducks and chickens and a turkey and lots of pigs, all different kinds. Tess liked the big black pig with the squashed-in face. There were people too, and an old-fashioned tractor with a trailer and hay bales you could take out. At the very bottom of the box Tess found a farmhouse with roses painted on it and real curtains.

It took a long time to set the farm out properly. Tess was about to put the cars back into the box when she noticed a small package she had missed. Inside was a dull brown pig with a long snout. She put it with the other pigs.

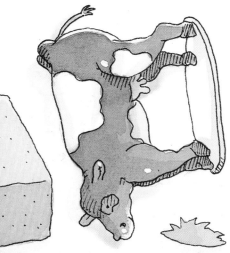

Dad was late that night and Tess was almost asleep when he came in to say good night.

"Look at your farm, Dad," said Tess.

"I've just been looking at it," said Dad. "That was Grandad's farm before it was mine. It's yours now; you take good care of it." Then Dad said something very peculiar: "WATCH OUT FOR TUSKER." At least that's what Tess thought he said.

The sun was shining when Tess woke up. She looked at the farm sitting in the middle of her messy room. Then she jumped out of bed. Something was wrong! She knelt down. Everything was wrong! The ducks were all huddled together in the sheep field, and the sheep were in the trailer. A cow was on its side on the farmhouse doorstep and the lady with the milking stool was lying on her back with her legs in the air. The chickens and the turkey had disappeared. Only the pigs were unchanged. They stood peacefully in their field just where Tess had left them. Their gate was slightly open and the dull brown pig was poking his long snout through the gap. Tess closed the gate and put the brown pig in the pigsty.

She found the chickens and the turkey under the tractor trailer. It almost looked as though they were hiding.

Tess put everything back the way it had been before. "You be good," she said. Then she went to find Nicky who lived next door. Nicky was older than Tess. He loved the farm. He built a haystack with the hay bales, and he showed Tess how to make a pond for the ducks out of kitchen foil.

Dad was very impressed with the new pond.

"Something happened last night," said Tess. "Something very bad." Dad shook his head. Then he said it again: "WATCH OUT FOR TUSKER."

"What do you mean?" demanded Tess. "Who is Tusker?"

"I don't know," said Dad. "It's something Grandad used to say to me."

Next morning, when Tess woke up, it had happened again, only worse. The bales from Nicky's haystack were all over the place and the trailer was tipped on its end. The big horses were upside-down in the duck pond and the foil was ripped. The cows and the sheep were crammed into the farmhouse, all on top of each other, and the people lay face down in the barn. The ducks and the chickens were on the farmhouse roof and the turkey was perched on the chimney. Fences and gates were everywhere.

"At least the pigs are all right," said Mum cheerfully. And so they were – in their field just where Tess had left them. But their gate was wide open, and the brown pig with the long snout was not in his sty. He was halfway across the sheep field.

29

"You are a bad pig," said Tess. She picked him up and looked at him curiously. "I didn't know pigs had tusks," she said. Then she remembered Dad's words – WATCH OUT FOR TUSKER.

"Let me have a look," said Mum. Tess handed her the dull brown pig with the long snout. "That's not a pig!" said Mum. "That's a wild boar. Wild boars don't live on farms: they're dangerous!"

Tess couldn't wait for Dad to come home. When she heard Dad's key in the front door, she rushed to meet him.

"I've found him!" she shouted.

"Found who?" said Dad, who was putting down his things.

"Tusker," said Tess. She opened her hand, and showed Dad the pig with the long snout and tusks. "Grandad's wild boar."

"Good heavens!" said Dad. He sat down at the kitchen table rather heavily. "Watch out for Tusker," he said almost to himself. "WATCH OUT FOR TUSKER," he said again a bit louder.

"He wasn't happy on the farm," said Tess.

"He wouldn't be," said Dad. "Tusker is a wild creature. He was probably frightened of all those gates and fences and machines and people."

At the bottom of the garden there was an overgrown patch that Mum and Dad called their wild garden. That was where Tess and Dad took Tusker. Tess put him gently down under an ivy leaf.

"Goodbye, Tusker," she said.

"Goodbye, Tusker," said Dad.

Next morning Tess woke up to find her farm exactly as she had left it. But Tusker had disappeared from under the ivy leaf. They never saw him again, but Tess was sure he was happy in the wild garden. And if ever anything went wrong – if a plant fell over, or a cabbage got nibbled, or a flowerpot got broken, someone was sure to say: WATCH OUT FOR TUSKER.

WHEN AM I GOING HOME?

Sally Grindley

Christopher's bed was right under the window. Sanjit's bed was on one side and Alice's was on the other. Christopher had been in hospital longer than Sanjit and Alice, and he was very fed up with lying in bed all day long.

"When am I going home?" he asked his mum every morning.

"When you're better," said his mum.

"When will that be?" he asked.

"Soon," said his mum. "Try to be patient."

But sometimes soon can seem like a very long time.

Christopher's favourite nurse was Nurse Ball. She was short and round and bouncy, just like a ball, and she always found time to spend with the children.

"You look in a right-down-in-the-dumps-misery-me sort of mood today," she said one morning.

"I'm bored," said Christopher, "and fed up, and I hate lying in this rotten old bed all day long."

"Rotten old bed!" exclaimed Nurse Ball, looking thoroughly shocked. "I'll have you know that's a magic bed you're lying in, young man."

"Don't be silly," said Christopher. "It's a rotten, old, hard hospital bed and I hate it."

"You mark my words," said Nurse Ball, "if you believe it's a magic bed, then a magic bed it will be. And magic beds can turn into anything and go anywhere you want them to."

"I don't believe you," Christopher laughed.

Nurse Ball just winked.

In the afternoon, after he had seen all the doctors and eaten his lunch, and before his dad came to visit, Christopher lay wishing something exciting would happen. He remembered what Nurse Ball had said about his bed and grinned. Part of him was sure that she was just pulling his leg, but another part of him thought how much fun he could have if only his bed were really magic. All the places he could go to ... All the things it could become ... Imagine whizzing through the air ... Imagine ...

Suddenly, he was at the wheel of a fire engine which was screaming along a road, siren blaring – NEE NA, NEE NA, NEE NA.

"Out of the way, idiot!" yelled Sanjit, who was sitting beside him, to the driver of a yellow car that was blocking the road. NEE NA, NEE NA, NEE NA.

In front of them they could see masses of black smoke billowing up into the sky, and bright orange flames dancing at the windows and skipping along the roof of an old warehouse. The fire engine screeched to a halt and Christopher and Sanjit jumped down. Other fire engines were already there, and the Fire Chief shouted at them to hurry up. They rushed towards the warehouse and directed their hoses at the burning windows. The heat from the flames knocked them back. It was scorching. Too hot to bear . . .

"Christopher, it's time for your medicine," a familiar voice came from close by. "What've you been up to, young man? You've got yourself all hot and bothered."

"I've been fighting a fire," said Christopher excitedly.

"Ah," said Nurse Ball. "I told you it was a magic bed."

Christopher's bed took him into the operating theatre the next day, and he didn't remember much after that.

But a few days later, when he was feeling much better and wishing he could go on another adventure, it took him across the world to see the elephants in Africa. It became a safari jeep which bumped and rattled its way through the parched savannah scrub.

"Look at those zebras!" yelled Alice above the noise.

"And there's a giraffe over there!" shouted Sanjit from the back.

As they drove through the next tangled mass of dusty bushes, they suddenly saw a large herd of elephants drinking at a small water hole.

"Wow!" said Christopher. "Just look at that huge mother elephant!"

"And look at the little baby one!" cried Alice. "I didn't know they could be so tiny."

"They're wonderful," said Sanjit.

It was Nurse Ball who drove away the elephants.

"You were miles away, Christopher. Another adventure?"

"I've just seen the elephants in Africa. They're beautiful."

"They certainly are," said Nurse Ball. "You're a lucky young man to have seen them. What's more, I've

good news for you. Your temperature's coming down, which means you're on the mend."

"Yippee!" yelled Christopher. "Does that mean I'm going home soon?"

"Just a little while longer," smiled Nurse Ball. "You might fit in one or two more adventures before you go. But don't tire yourself out."

Christopher's bed didn't stay still over the next two weeks. Every day, as soon as the doctors had examined him and after he had eaten his lunch, Christopher set off on a new adventure. His bed became a bulldozer and knocked over an old building. It flew him to Disney World to meet Mickey Mouse and Donald Duck. It drove him to school to visit all the friends he was missing while he was in hospital. It turned into a boat and took him deep sea fishing in the middle of the night. And it took him all the way to Scotland to eat crumpets in front of the fire with his grandparents.

Then, one afternoon, the bed became a hot air balloon. It was a beautiful day, the sun shining and clouds racing across the sky in the warm breeze. The pink, purple and red balloon swelled and swayed as Christopher filled it with the blasts of hot air that would raise it from the ground.

And they were off! Up and up! Higher and higher! Carried by the wind across the sky. Down below everything grew smaller and smaller until the cars looked like Christopher's toys and the houses like doll's houses.

"I can see my house!" yelled Christopher, "and look, there's my dad in the garden."

"My house is over there," yelled Alice. "The one with the red roof."

"And there's mine," shouted Sanjit, "just there by the park."

"I'm going to go home," said Christopher. "I'm going to go home. I'm going to go and see my mum and dad. Let's take the balloon down. Won't they be surprised?"

Christopher was fast asleep when his mum and dad came to see him at the hospital later that afternoon. They quietly packed his clothes into a bag and gently carried him to the car. When he woke up he found himself tucked up in his own bed in his own bedroom.

"Welcome home, son," said his delighted parents.

"So it really was a magic bed!" exclaimed Christopher. "Nurse Ball was right!"